P9-CQZ-494

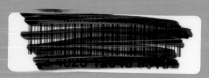

DATE DUE

JE 17 '11			
MR 2 1 '12			
AP 1 9 '12			
JE - - '12			
OC 3 0 '13			
MY 0 6 '14			
SE 2 9 '15			
JY 2 2 '16			
SE 0 5 '19			

All the water

a richard jackson book

atheneum books for young readers

new york london toronto sydney

in the world

by George Ella Lyon
and Katherine Tillotson

...is all the water

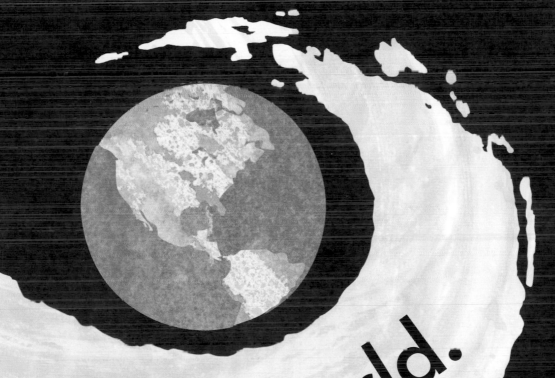

in the world.

Water

flows from the hose.

It wobbles

in blue pools.

It

fills

your

cup

up.

But where

does it come

from?

Water doesn't come.
It goes.
Around.

That rain

that cascaded from clouds

and meandered down mountains,

that wavered over waterfalls

then slipped into rivers

and opened into oceans,

that rain has been here before.

Thirsty air

    licks it from lakes

        sips it from ponds

            guzzles it from oceans

up
s
l
r
i
w
s

and this wet air

till it's crOWded into clouds

where it hangs hotly around

till cool air bumps through

and honey, those clouds

just

let

it

go

and

rain

rain

rain!

Tap dance

avalanche

stampede
of drips and drops and drumming—

a wealth of water.

Everything waits

for an open gate

in a wall of clouds

for rain sweet and loud

to fill the well

and start the stream.

for all to drink
use in tub or sink

wash in, splash in.

This wet wonder
means grow
      means life will flow

through tigers
through trees.

Through you

and through me.

All all

All together

all so precious—do not waste it.

And delicious—we can taste it.

Keep it clear, keep it clean . . .

keep Earth

green!

For Pete Seeger, Wendell Berry, Gurney Norman,
and all who work to save the water of life

And for Bernie Stoddard, who is just learning to swim in it
—G. E. L.

For Dick Jackson, dowser, editor, friend
—K. T.

ATHENEUM BOOKS
FOR YOUNG READERS
An imprint of Simon & Schuster
Children's Publishing Division
1230 Avenue of the Americas,
New York, New York 10020
Text copyright © 2011 by George Ella Lyon
Illustrations copyright © 2011 by Katherine Tillotson
ATHENEUM BOOKS FOR YOUNG READERS is a registered trademark of
Simon & Schuster, Inc. For information about special discounts for bulk
purchases, please contact Simon & Schuster Special Sales
at 1-866-506-1949 or business@simonandschuster.com.
The Simon & Schuster Speakers Bureau can bring authors to your live event.
For more information or to book an event, contact the Simon & Schuster
Speakers Bureau at 1-866-248-3049 or visit our website at
www.simonspeakers.com.
Book design by Ann Bobco
The text for this book is set in Neutraface.
The illustrations for this book are rendered digitally.
Manufactured in China • 1210 SCP
First Edition
1 2 3 4 5 6 7 8 9 10
Library of Congress Cataloging in Publication Data
Lyon, George Ella, 1949–
All the water in the world / George Ella Lyon ;
illustrated by Katherine Tillotson. — 1st ed. p. cm.
"A Richard Jackson book."
ISBN 978-1-4169-7130-6
1. Hydrologic cycle—Juvenile literature.
I. Tillotson, Katherine, ill. II. Title.
GB848.L96 2011
551.48—dc22
2010029530